PAN'S REALM

Don't miss any of the chilling adventures!

SPOOKSVILLE

PAN'S
REALM

Christopher Pike

Aladdin
NEW YORK LONDON TORONTO SYDNEY NEW DELHI

ALADDIN

An imprint of Simon & Schuster Children's Publishing Division
1230 Avenue of the Americas, New York, NY 10020
This Aladdin paperback edition July 2015
Text copyright © 1996 by Christopher Pike
Cover illustration copyright © 2015 by Vivienne To
Also available in an Aladdin hardcover edition.
All rights reserved, including the right of reproduction
in whole or in part in any form.
ALADDIN is a trademark of Simon & Schuster, Inc.,
and related logo is a registered trademark of Simon & Schuster, Inc.
For information about special discounts for bulk purchases,
please contact Simon & Schuster Special Sales at 1-866-506-1949
or business@simonandschuster.com.
Cover designed by Jessica Handelman
Interior designed by Mike Rosamilia
The text of this book was set in Weiss Std.
Manufactured in the United States of America 0615 OFF
2 4 6 8 10 9 7 5 3 1
Library of Congress Control Number 2015931897
ISBN 978-1-4814-1081-6 (hc)
ISBN 978-1-4814-1079-3 (pbk)
ISBN 978-1-4814-4302-9 (eBook)
This book was previously titled The Little People.

PAN'S REALM

1

THE GANG HAD NEVER GONE ON A REAL
picnic before. Not in a meadow with a proper basket of food and a blanket to lie on in the sun. It was
Cindy Makey who suggested it would be fun to do it
at least once before school started. And since no one
else could think of anything better to do that day, a
picnic it was.

Their town, Spooksville, was surrounded by moun-
tains and hills on three sides and the ocean on the
fourth. It was in these wooded hills that they decided
to have their picnic. There were many beautiful
meadows in these woods. Meadows isolated enough
that a person could pretend he or she was in the middle

of nowhere. Places where evil could happen, and no one would be the wiser.

Until it was too late.

"I hope you didn't put mayonnaise on my sandwich," Watch said as Cindy began to empty the picnic basket on the yellow blanket they had brought. The meadow was filled with bright yellow daisies with black centers. Nearby a stream gurgled and there wasn't a cloud in the sky. The surrounding trees were tall, heavy branched. Although they now sat in the sun, they had found the hike from the road through the woods rather chilly. The shadows were deep in these woods, and old.

"Since when did you care what's between two slices of bread?" Sally Wilcox asked Watch. "You used to be the most unpicky eater I know. Hey, Cindy, Adam—I remember the time Watch ate half a dozen uncooked eggs."

Cindy made a face and hooked her long blond hair behind her ears. "Is that true?" she asked Watch.

"It was at Easter, an egg-eating contest," Watch explained. "The eggs were painted different colors."

Sally smiled and pushed back her brown bangs. "So were the egg yolks. Only one had a normal yellow center. In fact, if I remember correctly, the one egg you didn't eat eventually hatched and out popped a small reptilian creature that burrowed in the ground and eventually ate most of the local gophers." Sally added, "I think the witch had something to do with those eggs."

"At least I won first prize in the contest," Watch said, fiddling with his pocket calculator. He was working out calculations for a new telescope he was building. Watch, in addition to wearing four watches, usually carried a calculator, just as Sally usually carried a Bic lighter.

"What was the prize?" Adam Freeman, who was the new kid in town, asked.

"A twenty-dollar gift certificate to the drugstore," Sally said. "For the next year Watch got to buy all the antacids he needed."

"The eggs did kind of make me sick," Watch agreed. He checked out the turkey sandwich Cindy had handed him through his thick glasses. "After that I kind of lost my taste for chicken as well as for eggs."

"Is the sandwich OK?" Cindy asked Watch, concerned.

Watch chewed noisily. "Yeah. I'm not as picky as Sally says. As long as nothing in it bites back, I don't really care what I eat."

Adam gestured to the picnic basket. "What kind of sandwich did you make me?"

Cindy beamed. "It's a surprise. You'll love it."

Sally was amused. "You'll both be surprised."

Cindy was annoyed. "You didn't change our sandwiches, did you?"

"Are you asking me or telling me?" Sally, who already had her plain cheese sandwich in hand, wanted to know.

"I don't believe this," Cindy said as she checked the remaining two sandwiches.

"What is it?" Adam asked, already losing his appetite.

"We both have Spam sandwiches," Cindy said, laying open the slices of bread for dark-haired Adam to see. "Spam and sprouts."

"What's wrong with that?" Watch asked. "I like Spam."

"I like sprouts," Sally said, laughing.

"Yeah," Cindy said sarcastically. "They really go perfectly together. Thanks a lot, Sally. After I went to all that trouble to make us all really nice sandwiches."

Sally spoke to Adam. "Don't believe a word of it. I saw your original sandwich. It looked like something for building strong bones and teeth rather than something you'd want to eat."

"If the Spam doesn't have mayonnaise on it," Watch said, "I'll eat it."

Cindy tossed the sandwiches aside. "They have *catsup* all over them."

"And little green things from an old jar at the back of the refrigerator," Sally added. "You didn't look under the Spam, Cindy dear."

Cindy scowled at Sally as she reached for the other basket. "Just for that you don't get any dessert. And I know you didn't fool with my chocolate cake because I didn't take my eyes off it."

"*After* you baked it," Sally said. "But what about *before?*"

"What did you put in it?" Cindy demanded.

Sally laughed. "Nothing."

"Except for a few of those little purple things from the back of the refrigerator," Watch added.

Adam swallowed. "I'm glad I had breakfast."

"Watch is kidding," Sally said. "The cake is fine—as long as Cindy didn't ruin it with all the sugar and *love* she poured into it. I know she was thinking of you, Adam, when she baked it."

"Better him than a complete stranger who wouldn't care if Cindy choked to death on the cake or not," Watch said wisely. "Are you sure you don't want your Spam sandwich?" Watch asked hungrily.

"Yeah, I'm sure." Cindy tentatively opened the picnic basket with the cake. "Seriously, I hope you didn't mess with this cake, Sally. I may be a lousy gourmet cook, but I do know how to bake."

"It doesn't take much of a cook or a baker to make sandwiches," Sally said.

"Shut up," Cindy said to Sally as she removed the cake from the basket. Adam—feeling a little hungry, his breakfast notwithstanding—leaned forward to get a better look. But he hardly had a chance to see what was left of his lunch, when a small green man, with a nose as long as a spoon and hands as quick as a fox, leapt out of the trees, grabbed the cake, and disappeared back into the woods.

The four of them blinked. They sat in stunned silence.

"Did you guys see what I just saw?" Sally finally asked.

Sure. They had all seen the same thing.

A leprechaun had stolen their chocolate cake.

FIVE MINUTES HAD PASSED SINCE THE LEP-
rechaun had appeared—and disappeared—and they
were still in shock. Well, perhaps *shock* was too strong
a word. After all, they had seen many strange and even
supernatural things in Spooksville. But they had never
lost a chocolate cake before.

"Are we sure we saw what we thought we saw?"
Cindy asked. "Maybe it was just a kid dressed up like a
leprechaun."

"No kid could move that fast," Watch said.

"Or be that ugly," Sally added.

"I thought he was kind of cute," Cindy said.

"You would," Sally said.

"It doesn't matter whether he was cute or ugly," Adam interrupted. "The fact is he was a leprechaun and we have to ask ourselves what leprechauns are doing in Spooksville."

"We have everything else," Watch said. "Why shouldn't we have leprechauns?"

"But why would he steal our cake?" Cindy asked.

"Probably because he was hungry," Sally said.

"I think Cindy means, why does he care about a cake?" Adam said. "Aren't leprechauns only worried about guarding their treasure, their pots of gold?"

"Their treasure can be anything: an old shoe, a ring, a hat," Watch said. "The main thing is that the treasure is special to them, and that they guard it with their lives."

"So, you're saying we now have a leprechaun with a chocolate cake for a treasure?" Adam asked.

"It looks like it," Watch said.

"Since when did you become an expert on leprechauns?" Sally asked

Watch shrugged. "It's useful in Spooksville to know a little about every kind of supernatural creature."

Cindy pouted. "But I want to have a piece of my cake. I made it to eat."

Sally laughed. "How can you be so attached to a cake?"

Adam stood. "I want to find this leprechaun, to talk to him."

Watch got up too. "Leprechauns are impossible to find unless they want to be found. You saw how fast he moved. He could be miles from here by now."

But Cindy was adamant that they go after him. "He won't move so fast with a big cake in his hands."

They entered the woods where the leprechaun had disappeared and found a path of sorts that was heavily overgrown with briars. They hadn't gone far when they were in deep shadow. Here the temperature was at least twenty degrees lower than it had been in the bright sun of the meadow. They were able to check it on a thermometer on one of Watch's four watches. In fact, it was while they were doing so that a leprechaun suddenly appeared in a tree above them, reached down, and grabbed that watch.

The creature was gone before they could move.

Watch was upset, which was rare for him. "He has our cake. He didn't need to steal one of my watches."

"That wasn't the same leprechaun," Sally said.

"How do you know?" Adam asked.

"He was older and had a wart on the end of his nose," Sally said.

"Then there are at least two of them," Cindy said. "There could even be dozens of them."

"Or thousands," Sally said darkly. "This could be the prelude to an invasion by leprechauns."

Adam was concerned. "Maybe it isn't such a good idea to chase after them. The forest is thick here. They could come at us from all sides. Maybe we should get back to our bikes and go for help."

The gang agreed. They headed back in the direction of the meadow. When they got there they discovered that their blanket and picnic baskets were also gone. Now it was Sally's turn to be angry.

"Those horrible little creatures," she said. "That was one of my mom's best blankets."

"How can you be so attached to a piece of cloth?" Cindy asked.

"Shut up," Sally snapped.

"Quiet, both of you," Adam interrupted before the girls could get going. "We better get back to the road as fast as possible. We'll be lucky if our bikes are still there."

Of course, their bikes were gone. The leprechauns had more than a few treasures now, and the gang had to wonder if the creatures would ever give them back.

"But we have to try to get our bikes back," Sally said. "Walking home will take us the rest of the day."

Adam spoke to Watch. "In all you've read about leprechauns, are they ever described as dangerous?" he asked.

Watch scratched his head. "They can get pretty mean if you steal their treasure. But they're usually so small, and have so little magic, that a human can handle one."

"But what about a dozen?" Cindy asked, worried.

"If you're scared you can stay here and guard the dirt," Sally suggested.

Cindy scowled at her but didn't say anything. Adam paced the spot where their bikes had been. "If we go back into the woods," he said, "we might lose more stuff."

"What else have we got to lose?" Sally asked.

"They might take another of my watches," Watch said.

"Or our clothes," Cindy said.

Sally shook her head. "They're not getting our clothes off."

"We don't know what they're capable of," Adam warned. "There's got to be some risk. But if we walk back to town now, we know we'll be safe."

"But for how long?" Sally asked. "What if they're working their way down into town. I say we confront them here and now and show them how tough we are."

After another five minutes of bickering, they decided they wouldn't hike all the way back to town without trying to get their bikes back. They figured the leprechauns wouldn't be able to move around very fast with the bikes in the thick woods. Of course, they had no idea how long their bikes had been gone. They may have been the first items stolen.

They hiked back toward the meadow and then moved off in the direction the original leprechaun had disappeared. Soon they were deep in the trees again, unable to find a path as they pushed their way through hanging branches and overgrown bushes. Nettles scratched at their faces and arms, and although it was cool in the shade, they began to sweat.

"I wish they had at least left us the lemonade," Sally grumbled.

"They're scavengers, that's for sure," Adam said.

A half hour later, when they were pretty sure they were lost, they wandered out of the woods and stumbled upon a cave. It wasn't a normal cave, though. Dug into the side of a low rock hill, the opening was lined with cut stones. There was no question about it—the place had been built.

"Do leprechauns dig into the earth?" Adam asked Watch.

Watch studied the carved stones. "Not in any of the books I've read. But I'm pretty sure leprechauns didn't have anything to do with making this cave. These are almost the size of boulders—a leprechaun wouldn't have been able to lift them."

"What are you saying?" Sally asked. "Who do you think made this cave?"

"I don't know," Watch said. "But these rocks were recently carved. This cave hasn't been here long."

"We were getting nowhere wandering around in the woods," Adam suggested. "I say we go inside and have a look."

"But we don't have flashlights," Sally argued.

"You can stay here if you're scared," Cindy replied.

Watch peered into the cave. "I see a faint yellow light. There might be torches of some kind in there."

It was finally decided that they'd enter the cave. It didn't take long for them to make it to the light source. There were lamps, carved from stone with dark candles inside. They were arranged neatly along the sides of the cave, every thirty feet, and gave off enough light to see by. Watch mentioned that leprechauns ordinarily didn't like fire.

"Then another kind of creature created this cave," Adam figured.

"It looks that way," Watch agreed.

"I love Spooksville," Sally said sarcastically. "Just when you thought it was safe to go back in the woods."

The tunnel continued on in a relatively straight line for about a quarter of a mile, then abruptly it opened up into a vast cavern. Here there were many burning lamps, running water, and the sound of hard stone being shaped by hand tools. The cavern was far from empty.

The place was filled with dwarfs.

3

THEY LOOKED LIKE CLASSIC CHILDREN'S-BOOK
dwarfs, which is to say they were short and stout, with
thick beards and grim faces. Each carried a number of
tools: heavy hammers, sharp chisels, and hacksaws.
They stopped working as the gang stumbled into their
space. The dwarfs' eyes were dark and deep set, and
they stared at them with both surprise and concern. Yet
the little people didn't appear to be hostile.

Adam cleared his throat. "Hello," he said. "We didn't
mean to interrupt your work. We're looking for a few
leprechauns who stole our bikes and picnic baskets.
They wouldn't have happened to have gone by this way,
would they?"

The dwarfs glanced at one another, then back at Adam. Clearly the little guys didn't understand English. Adam spoke in Watch's ear.

"What language do dwarfs speak?" he asked.

Watch shrugged. "They probably have their own language."

"I think they're cute," Cindy gushed.

"Wait till they cut off one of your legs with an ax," Sally muttered.

"If they'd wanted to hurt us, they would have done it by now," Adam said. He turned his attention back to the dwarfs, who continued to stare at them with their tools in hand. Adam had on a green shirt, so he pointed to it, then made a scurrying motion with his hands, trying to describe how quickly the leprechauns moved. He wasn't sure if he conveyed what he meant, but one of the older dwarfs pointed farther into the cave. Adam paused. "The leprechauns went that way?" he asked.

The old dwarf nodded.

"He doesn't know what you're saying," Sally muttered.

"He might," Adam said hopefully. "We probably should keep going. It couldn't hurt."

"That's what we said about the Haunted Cave," Sally warned.

Since the dwarfs ignored them and went back to work, they did continue into the tunnel. But now it began to curve, and then forked in several places. Just as they were worried they were lost, the cave suddenly ended and they were back in the forest. But not at the same place they had entered the cave.

The forest had changed.

Now it was filled with more than trees.

There was a palace dead ahead, but not a palace in the usual sense of the word. This palace was made of grass and sticks, of bark and leaves. Yet it was so huge, so elaborate, that it resembled a castle more than a hut. The whole structure stirred as the wind swept through the trees. The building didn't look as if it had been there long, nor did it look as if it would last. There wasn't a soul in sight.

"Could the dwarfs have built this?" Cindy asked.

"Dwarfs work with stone and metal and jewels," Watch said. "They like to be underground. They'd never have built this."

"What about the leprechauns?" Sally asked.

Watch shook his head. "Leprechauns try to stay hidden so no one can find them. They wouldn't build such an obvious and big place."

"But it's empty," Cindy said.

"It might just appear to be empty," Adam warned. "I don't see anyone but I feel like we're being watched."

Sally nodded. "So do I. I think we should get out of here."

"And go where?" Cindy asked.

"Let Watch and me explore the palace," Adam suggested. "You girls stay here."

"No way," Sally said. "We go where you go. Right, Cindy?"

Cindy nodded without enthusiasm.

They crept into the palace, actually into a courtyard. It was as wide across as a football field and lined with branches and vines and decorated with multicolored flowers. There was a fountain in the center of the courtyard, and the water splashed out of a block of stacked stones and then collected in a sunny pool. They sat beside it and had a long drink. They were all so thirsty.

Then everything changed.

First the sky dimmed and took on a greenish hue. Then they heard a faint whistle echoing in the various rooms of the palace. The sound came at them from all sides. It was definitely not caused by the wind because there was a rhythm to it. Also, its source seemed to shift as they tried to pinpoint it. Then it was as if the very air itself began to change, to fill with faint figures that seemed to be made of sunlight and mist. It was impossible to focus on them, to be sure they were there.

"What's happening?" Cindy asked, nervous.

"They look like ghosts," Sally said darkly.

"They're not ghosts," Watch explained. "Ghosts don't build green palaces in the middle of the forest."

"Did you notice that we didn't see a thing until we drank the water?" Adam said.

"Do you think it was poisoned?" Sally asked, glancing at the fountain.

"It could have had something in it besides poison," Watch said. "Wait a second. Something's happening."

The ghostly figures vanished as the sky darkened more. It took on a purple color now. The whistling abruptly stopped, and an eerie silence filled the courtyard. They anxiously waited for something dreadful to happen.

They didn't have long to wait.

A figure appeared at the doorway of the courtyard, at the same place they had entered. It wore a dark-hooded robe, which hung low over its head and cast a shadow across its face. The figure was tall, thin, and in its right hand it carried a glowing green crystal.

"Oh no," Sally moaned.

It walked toward them.

4

THE GANG WAITED. THERE SEEMED TO BE
no point in running, no place to hide. The figure moved
stiffly as if there were only bones under that dark robe.
Yet after it stopped in front of them and threw back its
hood, they found themselves staring up at a beautiful
woman. Her hair was blond, with red highlights, and
her eyes were so green they seemed to sparkle with the
light from the crystal she held. For a long time she stared
down at them, her expression serious but not frightening. She didn't smile, nor welcome them in any way.
When she finally did speak, her voice was little more
than a whisper, not unlike the sound the wind makes as
it moves through the leaves.

"Why have you entered our home?" she asked.

"We're sorry," Adam said quickly. "We were just looking for the leprechauns who stole our bikes."

"There are no leprechauns here," the woman said.

"That's fine," Sally replied, trying to edge her way to the doorway. "We'll just be on our way." She grabbed Adam's shirt sleeve. "Come on, let's go."

"Wait," the woman said. "You drank our water."

"Just a little," Adam said, following Sally and the others as they slowly made their way around the woman. "We were thirsty. We're sorry if that's a problem."

"Humans should not drink fairy water," the woman said.

Adam stopped. "Is that what you are? A fairy?"

"What did you think I was?" the woman asked.

Watch shrugged. "You look like a woman to us."

At that the woman's face darkened. "A fairy never likes to be compared to a human. It annoys us and it's rude, especially to say such a thing in our own house."

"We're sorry," Adam said for what felt like the third time. "We meant you no harm. We'll be on our way now and we won't bother you again."

With his friends, Adam turned to leave. But just then the fairy woman held up the hand that held the green crystal and the light of the object began to increase dramatically. Pretty soon all they could see was green light, and they were stumbling over one another as they tried to get to the exit. Adam had to shut his eyes—the light was that blinding.

Then it stopped. A switch could have been thrown, it was that sudden. For a full minute Adam blinked his eyes to focus them. The sky had returned to its familiar blue, and the fairy had disappeared. Everything appeared perfectly normal, but Adam should have known better. He was dealing with a fairy, after all.

It took him another moment to realize his friends were gone.

Or were they?

"Sally?" he called. "Watch? Cindy?"

"Adam?" Watch called. "Where are you?"

"I'm right here. Where are you?"

"I'm right here," Watch said. "But you and the others must be invisible."

"I'm not invisible," Adam heard Sally say. "You guys are invisible."

"I think we're all invisible," Cindy said.

"That's it," Adam said. "She must have used magic on us. Let's go stand together on the first step of the doorway. At least we'll be able to touch."

But Adam was wrong. Even though they stood right

next to one another on the same step, they couldn't touch. Adam began to worry that they might be invisible for the rest of their lives.

"Maybe if we leave this fairy palace we'll be all right," Sally suggested. "Maybe the magic only works in here."

They tried that, and the situation actually got worse. Because as soon as they stepped outside the place, they began to have trouble hearing. Watch insisted they return inside.

"Because if we can't even talk to each other," he said, "then we're bound to get lost."

They hurried back inside.

"Did she turn us into fairies?" Cindy asked. "Is that the problem?"

"I don't think so," Adam said. "She seemed to think fairies were much better than humans, and I doubt that she would do us a favor by making us into her own kind."

"I agree," Watch said. "This is some kind of spell."

"So what have you read about fairy spells?" Sally asked.

"That they're a pain in the butt," Watch said.

"That's helpful," Cindy muttered.

"There must be some way to counteract the spell," Adam said. "I mean, fairies aren't supposed to be all that powerful."

Watch agreed. "There is usually a trick to breaking any spell. It's often something simple, like walking backward or holding your breath or spinning in circles."

"Why don't we try all those things?" Cindy asked.

So they did, but they only ended up feeling dizzy and out of breath. They still couldn't see or touch one another. Yet without warning, Adam caught sight of somebody's skin. The vision lasted only a second.

"Who was that?" he called.

"Who was what?" Sally asked.

"I saw a piece of somebody," Adam said.

"Who was it?" Cindy asked.

"I don't know," Adam said. "It was just a couple of inches of somebody's face."

"You should be able to tell my face from the others," Sally said.

"Maybe the things we just tried are working," Cindy said. "Maybe they just take time."

They waited for a few minutes to see if that was the case. But Adam saw no more slices of flesh pop out of the air.

"Maybe we should spin some more," Cindy said finally.

"I don't think that's it," Adam said. "Let's examine what each of us was doing at the instant I saw that piece of someone's face."

"I was scratching my face," Cindy said.

"You were probably picking your nose," Sally muttered.

"That's not true!" Cindy snapped. "I never do that in public."

"Now you can," Sally said.

"Stop arguing," Adam interrupted. "This is serious. What were you doing, Sally?"

"Just standing here."

"You must have been doing something besides that," Adam said.

"I was breathing," Sally said. "And picking my nose. What were you doing?"

Adam paused. "Nothing. I was just standing too. What were you doing, Watch?"

"Wiping my glasses," he said.

Adam jumped. "That's it! The glass in the glasses must be the key. I actually saw two small pieces of skin, each as large as your lenses. Watch, give me your glasses."

"Where are you?"

"I'm over here," Adam said. "No, wait, that won't work. We can't touch. But let's think about this. What if when light passes through glass it shows our skin?"

"Then why can't we see Watch's eyes right now?" Sally asked. "I assume he has his glasses on."

"I do," Watch said.

"But Watch always walks around with his head sort of down," Adam said. "Watch, take off your glasses and hold them up to the sun. Look up as well, so that your face is right behind them."

Watch must have done what he was told.

His nose and upper lip suddenly appeared.

"It works!" Cindy exclaimed.

The pieces of skin vanished.

"It must only work while the sun is shining on those two spots," Sally said. "The effect isn't permanent."

"But I think we're on the right track," Adam said. "What we need is a bigger piece of glass so our whole bodies can become visible at the same time. Then the effect might remain, and we could see each other again."

"That makes sense." Watch said.

"It does?" Sally asked.

"We're dealing with fairy magic here," Adam said. "The principle is what counts."

"But we're not going to find a huge piece of glass out here in the forest," Sally said.

"We might not have to, though," Watch said. "Like you said, Adam, it's the principle that matters. Rather than stand in light that has been filtered through glass, what if we stand in light that has been reflected? In that situation we'd also have light that has been slightly altered."

"As we've been slightly altered," Adam added.

"But where are we going to find a huge mirror out here in the middle of fairyland?" Sally asked.

"We don't need a mirror to find reflected light," Watch said. "The water from the fountain collects into a pool of water. Let's stand to the right side of it, on those rocks."

"I don't want to get near that water," Sally said. "It's what started our troubles."

"Fine," Cindy said. "Stay invisible for the rest of your life. Then we won't have to look at you anymore."

But Sally must have ignored her because a moment later—as they climbed onto the rocks beside the pool— the four of them suddenly became visible. Not only that, but they were able to touch one another, and none of them looked any the worse for wear.

"But we could disappear the moment we step out of this reflected light," Sally said.

"No. Once you break a fairy spell," Watch said, "it's broken."

To prove his point, he jumped off the rocks and moved away from the pool. He remained visible.

"Good," Adam said. "Let's get out of here before that fairy woman comes back."

"Yeah, I didn't like her," Sally said. "She was creepy."

"Like this is the best place in the whole world to insult her," Cindy said as they hurried toward the entrance of the fairy palace.

5

THEY WERE AFRAID TO RETURN TO THE dwarf cave because they had taken so many turns underground that they thought they'd get lost and have to remain in the dark. Walking out in the sun, even if it was under the trees and in the neighborhood of a bunch of fairies and leprechauns, seemed safer. But they were still lost. They had never been in these hills, in this part of the woods, and even when they climbed higher they weren't able to catch a glimpse of the city or the ocean.

"Whose idea was this picnic anyway?" Sally grumbled.

"Whose idea was it to confront leprechauns and show them how tough we are?" Cindy asked.

"It's weird how we've seen so many magical creatures

all at once," Adam said. "Usually, when we have an adventure, we deal with only one creature at a time. But now it's like a doorway has opened to another dimension, and the elementals are moving in."

"What are elementals?" Cindy wanted to know.

"Any kind of a nature spirit," Watch answered quickly. "And I don't think it's good we're seeing so many of them. Look how much trouble we've had already, and we're used to dealing with aliens and monsters and demons. What if normal people ran into these creatures?"

"I always think of myself as normal," Sally said.

"We all have our illusions," Cindy answered simply.

"But there must be a reason for all these creatures showing up all at once," Adam said. "Maybe if we figure out what it is, they'll all go home and leave us in peace."

Just then a voice seemed to speak from the sky.

"We can't go home."

The four of them almost jumped out of their skins. The voice was thick with power, clearly not human. It didn't sound angry, however, only a little sad. Adam cautioned the others to remain silent while he searched the immediate area. Yet no one was visible. Finally he stared up at the sky, spoke to it.

"Who's there?" he asked.

The voice replied, "Pan."

"Oh no," Watch said.

"Who's Pan?" Sally whispered.

"The king of the elementals," Watch said. "He's supposed to be very powerful."

"But is he evil?" Cindy asked.

"It depends on your definition of evil," Watch said.

"I'm not that bad," the voice answered.

"Where are you?" Adam asked. "Can we see you?"

"Do we want to see you?" Sally muttered.

"Continue the way you're going," the voice said. "I am not far. I will talk to you when you arrive."

Adam and Watch started to move, but Sally jumped in front of them. "Wait a second," she said, "this guy sounds like the big boss."

"That's good," Watch said. "He's the perfect one to tell us what's going on."

"He's the perfect one to turn us into toads," Sally said. "I say we run the other way, and not look back."

Adam shook his head. "We can't leave this mystery unsolved. Also, we have nowhere to go." He paused. "I think I remember reading a little about Pan. He plays the flute, doesn't he? He can't be all bad."

"He plays Pan pipes," Watch said. "Not a flute."

"Same difference," Adam continued. "It's not like he's a demon or a troll or something really evil."

"I don't like meeting supernatural creatures deep in the woods," Sally said. "It just isn't right."

But Sally's arguments fell on deaf ears. It was clear to the others that they had nowhere else to go. Finally they continued along the path, with Sally bringing up the rear. As Pan had said, it was not long before they reached him.

He stood in the center of a small clearing beside a stone wall with a brook nearby. He was half goat, half man. From his waist down he was animal-like—he had four legs, ending in cloven hoofs. Above the waist he was a man and an extremely handsome one too. He was about forty with a dark goatlike beard. Atop his head, though, he had two black horns. In one hand he carried his famous Pan pipes, although he didn't look like he was in the mood for music. He glanced up as they came into the meadow but then hung his head. He appeared to be in deep thought or else was depressed.

"Hello," he said in his magical way. The word echoed all around them, even though he hadn't raised his voice.

"Hi," Adam said. "I'm Adam and these are my friends, Cindy and Watch and Sally."

"I know who you are," he said.

"Really?" Adam said. "How?"

"I have watched you since you entered this forest.

I do not have to be near you to see you. I know your names, and I know how you feel and how you think."

"Please don't judge me by today," Sally said quickly. "I haven't been at my best."

"She's usually worse," Cindy muttered.

"Are we disturbing you?" Adam asked, wondering why Pan continued to hang his head and not look at them.

"No," he said. "It doesn't matter."

"What doesn't matter?" Watch asked.

"Nothing matters," Pan replied quietly. "Not anymore."

"Why not?" Adam asked. "What's happened?"

Pan sighed. "It's a long story."

"We like stories," Sally said brightly. "In fact, I might be an author when I grow up. Maybe we could take down your story and get it published. You can get royalties and advances and all kinds of money these days. You might even get a movie deal, being a supernatural creature and all."

But Pan just shook his head. "This is a sad story. No one will want to read it."

"You're wrong there," Sally said. "Half the adult population in this country suffers from depression. They love sad stories, particularly when they have unexpected endings."

But Pan wasn't interested. "You don't understand. No one understands."

Adam stepped forward so that he was not more than ten feet from Pan. It was only as he got closer that he realized the king of the elementals was really much larger than a normal person. Yet not for a moment did Adam feel afraid. Obviously Pan was too absorbed in what was happening in his own life to harm four kids.

"We would like to understand," Adam said. "Please tell us your story. We're good listeners. And who knows, we might be able to help you."

Pan sighed again. "Very well, I will tell you. Sit here on the grass beside me. That way if you get bored, you can lie down and take a nap."

"Why do you think we'll get bored?" Cindy asked as she sat down beside Adam.

"Other people's problems are always boring," Pan said.

"Not to me," Sally said. "I thrive on them."

Pan looked up and smiled faintly. He had a nice smile. "I have watched you the closest since you entered these woods," he said. "You always have something smart to say."

"Better smart than stupid," Sally replied.

"I'm afraid I've been more of the latter lately," Pan said.

And taking a deep breath, he started his tale.

6

As you have already guessed, all my elementals have moved into your world. We came through an interdimensional portal not far from here. It opens and closes at my command. But what you don't know is that none of us wants to be here. We have come only because we have lost our homes."

"How?" Adam asked.

Pan hung his head again and spoke softly. "In my realm there is a powerful wizard named Klandor, who has been bothering me for centuries. I haven't been able to force him out of my kingdom because he knows many spells, and besides, I don't like to shove people around, even if they are wizards. He has been trying to take over my position since I can remember. Even though he is a wizard, nobody would do what he commanded unless he threatened to harm them. In my realm I was king. When I gave an order it was obeyed. That drove Klandor crazy with envy."

"It would bug me," Sally remarked.

Pan continued. "About a month ago I decided to hold a huge feast. It was my birthday, and, anyway, I like to hold feasts and eat a lot and play my pipes. Every musician loves an audience. I did not invite Klandor, but he arrived anyway. I did not ask him to leave, not in front of my guests. As I said, I'm polite and don't lose my temper unless pushed to the limit. Klandor walked in as if he owned the place and sat down and immediately insulted a couple of my dwarfs, who had never liked him. I told the dwarfs to ignore him and maybe he would go away."

"You aren't as forceful as you're portrayed in the books," Watch interrupted, "and why do you have four legs? In all the paintings I've seen, you've had only two legs."

"Those paintings are more modern. I've always had four legs." A note of pride entered Pan's voice. "And I can be forceful when it suits me. But let me get back to what happened that night."

"Please do," Adam said.

"Toward the end of the party, when we were stuffed with food and getting drowsy, Klandor brought out an old gold coin. He suggested we enjoy a harmless game, where we wagered small things. He even said I could flip the coin in the air and call heads or tails, which sounded fair to me. I mean, I didn't see how he could cheat me if I was tossing the coin."

"But he's a wizard," Adam said. "It might have been a magical coin."

Pan shrugged. "It sounded harmless to me. We were going to wager only small items: a silver plate from my table, a copper ring from his treasury, a silk robe from my closet, a crystal necklace from his study. He had brought his items with him so when I won something, he gave it to me right away. And I did the same—I have always paid my debts promptly."

"What did you win?" Cindy asked.

Pan brightened. "Lots of things at first. I won most of what he brought. But then my luck turned. I would call heads, and it would be tails. I would say tails, and it would be heads. Really, I had an extraordinary run of bad luck. I think I lost twenty bets in a row. In fact, I lost back to him almost everything I had won. My servants were kept busy bringing goods from my rooms to meet my debts. I eventually emptied my house, and I have a big castle."

"Wait a second," Watch interrupted. "You said you were only betting small things?"

Pan looked more depressed. "At first we were, but then Klandor kept betting me double or nothing. I had to match everything he had already won from me, each time I tossed the coin. One of two things could happen. If I could win just once, I would be even. But every time I lost, I lost a great deal."

"And with each bet, the stakes went way up," Adam said.

"Exactly," Pan answered. "But I kept thinking I had to win at least once, and then everything would be all right. But I never did. The coin always landed opposite from what I called."

"But you didn't bet your kingdom away?" Sally asked. "That would have been completely stupid."

Pan looked as miserable as a half-goat, half-man creature could. "Well," he said sadly, "yes, I did. I lost it all."

Adam tried to sound cheerful. "We all make mistakes."

"But not all of us make such big mistakes," Watch added.

"But how can you lose a kingdom with a toss of a coin?" Cindy asked. "I don't understand."

"Everyone was watching the game," Pan explained. "I couldn't refuse to hand over my kingdom. I had lost it fair and square." He sighed. "My poor elves, dwarfs, gnomes, leprechauns, fairies—as soon as Klandor took over he ordered us out. I guess he wanted to get back at all the elementals for ignoring him while I was king."

"Why did you come here?" Watch asked.

Pan shrugged. "We didn't know where else to go. This seemed as good a place as any."

"But your elementals can't stay here," Sally said. "They cause too much trouble. Your leprechauns stole our bikes and our picnic stuff. And one of your fairies made us invisible. Even in Spooksville, you can't get away with stuff like that and not suffer repercussions."

"I can get your bikes back for you," Pan said quickly.

"I'm missing a watch as well," Watch said.

"Leprechauns have a thing for watches," Pan admitted. "But I will do everything in my power to make sure yours is returned." He glanced at Cindy. "But they have probably eaten your chocolate cake by now."

Cindy smiled. "That's OK. I lost my appetite when the fairy turned us invisible."

"Yes, but that was a simple spell to break." Pan hung his head again. "Your troubles are easily solved."

"But there must be some way to win your kingdom back," Adam said.

Pan shook his head. "It's gone. I have to learn to accept that."

"You say you lost your kingdom fair and square," Adam continued, ignoring his defeatist attitude. "How do you know Klandor didn't cheat you?"

"How could he cheat?" Pan asked. "I was the one tossing the coin."

"But the odds against losing twenty coin tosses in a row is thousands to one," Watch said. "He must have cheated. Also, the fact that he brought stuff to wager means that he'd planned to play the game."

Pan was interested. "Those are good points. I have, of course, thought of them myself. But unless I can prove that Klandor cheated, there is no way to get my kingdom back. I can't simply accuse him, he'd just laugh in my face." Pan turned his head away. "He laughed at me as he ordered me to leave my castle."

"That's so sad," Cindy said sympathetically.

"I would never gamble away my entire kingdom," Sally muttered.

"You'll never have a kingdom," Cindy told her. "You'll

be lucky if you can afford your own apartment when you get older."

"You'll probably be a homeless wretch," Sally snapped back. "You'll be like Bum, hanging out at the beach and feeding the birds."

"Whatever happens to me, I'll be happy," Cindy retorted. "Not like you. You're going to end up in a mental hospital for people who think they're important when they're as insignificant as rocks."

"They always carry on like this," Watch explained to Pan. But Pan was too lost in his own problems to take much notice.

"Gambling has always been a weakness with me," he admitted.

"I am confused by a remark you made," Adam said to Pan. "You said, 'In fact, I lost back to him *almost* everything I had won.'" Adam paused. "Did he let you keep anything you'd won?"

Pan paused. "He let me keep his crystal necklace."

"Why?" Watch asked.

Pan shrugged. "Maybe he felt sorry for me."

"Klandor doesn't sound like a 'feel sorry for' kind of guy," Sally remarked.

"Did you wear this necklace while you were making your bets?" Adam asked.

Pan nodded. "I had it around my neck. I won it near the beginning, when I was winning things."

Adam and Watch gave each other knowing looks. "Did Klandor suggest you put it on?" Watch asked.

Pan had to strain to remember. "Now that you mention it, I think he encouraged me. Yes, I remember now he said how nice the crystal went with my two horns." He paused. "But what does the necklace have to do with losing my kingdom?"

"Did you start to lose after you put on the necklace?" Adam asked.

"Yes," Pan said reluctantly. "But I lost before I put it on as well."

"What Adam is asking," Watch said, "is if you lost a lot before you put on the necklace? Naturally you'd lose some with or without the necklace."

Pan was troubled. "It's hard to remember everything that happened that night because it was so upsetting. But it does seem that after I put on the necklace, I lost a lot more."

"Did you win *any* bets after you put it on?" Adam asked.

"I'm not sure," Pan said. "But I don't think so."

"Why can't you be sure?" Sally insisted.

Pan was puzzled. "It is strange. Usually my memory is very good. For example, I can remember all my human friends from thousands of years ago. When you're immortal, you don't forget things easily."

"It's possible the necklace made you forget," Watch said.

"It's possible it did much more than that," Adam said. "I'm sure Watch is thinking the same thing I am. The necklace might have changed what you thought you were seeing."

"Is this possible?" Cindy asked.

"We're dealing with an evil wizard here," Sally told her. "Those guys can and will do anything."

"Let me ask you another question," Adam said. "Could any of your elemental friends see the coin when it landed?"

"They were gathered around us," Pan said. "The party was in the main hall of my castle. But my friends were not that close." He paused. "Only Klandor and I could actually see if the coin landed tails or heads."

"Did Klandor want it this way?" Watch asked.

Pan hesitated. "Yes."

"He arranged it this way before you started betting?" Adam asked.

"Yes. The coin landed on a deep cushion placed between us, and it was his cushion that we used."

"Do you have your crystal necklace with you?" Adam asked.

"Somewhere," Pan answered. "But I don't know exactly where. I tossed it away after I lost my kingdom. I didn't want to wear anything that reminded me of Klandor."

"Understandable," Cindy said.

"Why do you want the necklace?" Sally asked Adam.

"I want to try it on," Adam said. "I want to see if it makes me see the opposite of what I want to see."

"I don't understand," Pan said.

"Every time you tossed the coin," Adam explained, "you wanted it to land either heads or tails. Like you said, you called out your choice while the coin was in the air. But what if the crystal necklace made your eyes or your mind work so that no matter what way the coin landed, you saw it opposite from what you had called?"

Pan was thoughtful. "Are you saying I was tricked out of my kingdom?"

"We've been saying that all along," Sally replied.

"It was more than a trick," Adam said. "He used a magical device against you. What we have to do now is find that necklace, and test it."

"I left it in my old kingdom," Pan said. "I tossed it somewhere along the road."

"Can we get back into your kingdom?" Watch asked.

Pan nodded. "There is a portal located not far from here."

"But it doesn't sound like we'll be able to find this necklace," Cindy said. "Unless you know exactly where you tossed it."

Pan scratched his head. "I have an idea. If we search together, we should be able to find it. And we can always bring a few leprechauns with us. Those guys can find anything."

"We would rather leave the leprechauns behind, if you don't mind," Sally said.

"But even if we do find the necklace and prove that it makes you see things opposite from the way you want them to be, that proof is not necessarily going to win Pan back his kingdom," Watch said. "Klandor can always refuse to give it back."

Pan nodded grimly. "Klandor is not the fairest wizard in the world."

"Let's worry about that when the time comes," Adam suggested. "The first thing is to find the necklace and see if our theory is right. Once we prove that, we can make plans to get the kingdom back."

Pan was touched. "You would do all this for me? And I have done nothing for you?"

"Well, I am hoping to get my watch back," Watch said.

Adam stood and brushed off his pants. "We're used to helping strange creatures. We run into them all the time."

Sally also stood. "Yeah, as long as the creature isn't trying to kill us, we help him."

PAN LED THEM TO AN INCREDIBLY HUGE pine tree that stood by itself in a meadow in the woods. The pine was surrounded by grass but nothing else, not a bush, not another small tree. The circular meadow was two hundred feet across. It almost looked as if it were regularly attended to. The lawn was manicured. Maybe the leprechauns mowed it every week—that was Sally's opinion, even though Pan did not confirm it. The king of the elementals gestured to the area as they walked up to the tree.

"Are you familiar with interdimensional portals?" he asked.

"Oh yeah," Adam said. "There's one in our town cemetery. We've been to a couple of different dimensions."

"Neither of which was very pleasant," Sally added.

"This portal opens only into the realm of the elementals," Pan explained. "It's a beautiful place, or at least it was when I was king. But now that Klandor is in charge I have no idea how things have changed. Anyway, we enter my old kingdom by starting at the edge of the circular meadow and walking backward around the tree seven times. With each revolution, we move a few feet closer to the tree. The last circle will be the shortest. Do you understand?"

Sally waved her hand. "Piece of cake." She turned to Cindy. "I suppose you'll have some excuse to stay behind. A sudden attack of the flu perhaps? Or else a nose bleed coming on?"

Cindy scowled. "I feel fine, thank you, and I'm looking forward to seeing this other dimension. But if you want to stay behind and keep looking for your *baby blanket*, I won't judge you."

"Do leprechauns ever fight like this?" Watch asked Pan.

"Only when their treasures are stolen," Pan replied.

Together, with Pan leading, they began to walk backward around the tree. Despite having four legs, which he had to use in reverse, Pan was a smooth mover. But Adam found it hard to keep his legs moving backward. Seven revolutions around the tree were a lot. By the time they neared the tree, he was feeling tired and sore. He wasn't even sure which was the seventh turn. For that reason the switch into the other dimension caught him completely by surprise.

They were in the meadow and then they were in deep space.

There were burning stars, shimmering nebulas, spinning planets. All these seemed to be turning on some giant invisible axis. In black outline he could see his friends and Pan nearby. It was almost as if they stood, for a moment, at the center of the universe. Then there was a flash of white light and Adam found himself falling.

But he didn't fall far and landed on a soft carpet of grass in a new dimension lit by a soft blue light. As Adam rolled he realized that Pan's realm did not mirror the forest outside Spooksville as the other dimensions he had entered had mirrored Spooksville.

Pan's kingdom was much grander. They were still in a meadow, true, but the surrounding trees were ten times taller than ordinary trees. Not far away were thundering waterfalls and mountain peaks that seemed to reach the sky. Even the flowers in the bushes were more spectacular, large and radiant with colors squeezed from rainbows. Yet over all a soft blue glow shone. The light seemed to come out of the matter itself, from the blades of grass, even from the dirt. Pan smiled as he looked around, perhaps it was good to be home. He gestured with a wide sweep of his arm.

"All this was mine," he said.

"Those were expensive coin tosses," Sally said, obviously impressed by the splendor of the dimension. She pointed to a distant mountain peak that rose straight up like an arrow aimed at the stars. "Have you ever climbed to the top of that, Pan?"

"When I was a young man," he said proudly. "I am the only person in this entire realm to scale it. It's called the Point. It reaches all the way into outer space."

"Cool," Watch said.

Adam was concerned. "This is a nice place but it's so big. Is your castle far from here? We want to help you defeat the evil wizard, but we'd also like to be home in time for dinner."

"I have to cook tonight," Cindy added.

"It is not far," Pan reassured them. "We should be able to walk there in less than two hours. It was along the road between here and there that I threw away the crystal necklace."

"Then let's hit the road," Sally said "The sooner we get rid of Klandor—and those nasty leprechauns—the happier I'll be."

"Leprechauns are not so bad once you get to know them," Pan said as they stepped onto a wide dirt road that led through the trees. "They're just boisterous."

"There are many kids in the prisons across our country who would say the same thing," Sally said.

"There are a few people on death row who would also say the same thing," Watch added.

They had gone about a mile when they were attacked.

Arrows flew out of the trees. One struck Watch in the calf before they knew what was happening. Letting out a painful cry, Watch crumpled to his knees and grabbed his leg. Adam knelt down beside him.

"Can you walk?" Adam asked.

Watch shook his head, trying to pull the arrow out. Already the blood was staining his pants leg. "No. Take cover, save yourselves."

The arrows continued to fly from the woods.

One struck Sally in her hair, where it got caught, and almost caused her to faint. Cindy hurried to Watch's side and tried to help him up.

"We have to get him off the road!" she cried.

"It hurts too much!" Watch moaned. "Leave me.

"We won't leave you," Pan said, reaching down with a strong arm. "Help him onto my back before another of their arrows hits us."

Adam and Cindy lifted Watch under his arms and managed to get him onto Pan's back. Without another word they all dashed into the woods on the opposite side of the road from the flying arrows. The trees were so dense—they were able to hide quickly. They helped Watch off Pan's back and set him down on the moist earth. Crouching behind thick bushes, they peered back the way they had come. The arrows had stopped, and for the moment the attack seemed over. Pan bent over and studied Watch's wound. The arrow was still stuck in Watch's leg, but the bleeding was not too bad. Pan shook his head sadly.

"We were attacked by elves," he said. "This is an elf arrow."

"But I thought you said all the elementals followed you into Spooksville's forest?" Adam asked.

Pan was grim. "Most of them did. But a few didn't want to leave their lands and were allowed to stay by swearing allegiance to Klandor. The evil wizard probably set them to guard the road beside the portal just in case I did return."

"We have to get this arrow out," Cindy cried, sitting beside Watch and holding his hand. "It's hurting him."

"It will hurt worse to pull it out," Pan warned. "And then the wound will bleed more." He studied Watch. "But it will have to come out soon if it's not to cause any permanent damage. Do you trust me to operate on you, Watch?"

Watch grimaced. "I trust you more than I trust Sally and Adam."

"I have no plans to be a doctor when I grow up," Sally joked, although it was clear she was shaken by the sudden attack, and by the injury to her good friend.

"Even with the arrow out," Pan said, "Watch won't be able to walk for some time."

"Then we have to go back," Cindy said "We tried and it didn't work out. What can we do?"

Pan raised his head and looked back in the direction they had come from. "I had resigned myself to never reclaiming my kingdom. That is until I met you four and you gave me hope. It is hard to let go of that hope, now that I have finally found it." But then he sighed and lowered his head. "But you are not my subjects. I have no right to lead you into deeper danger."

"It does seem that we have to go back," Adam said.

"I agree," Sally said. "We have no idea how many more of those nasty elves are patrolling these woods."

But Watch suddenly spoke up. "No. You can't abandon the quest this easily. Pan, take the arrow out and give me something to bandage the wound. I'll rest here until you return."

Pan was grave. "The elves who shot at us might find you and kill you. Klandor has obviously twisted their minds. You would be helpless lying here."

"I'll stay with him," Cindy said. "I'll guard him."

Sally was impressed. "That's very brave of you." She added, "Or else it's very stupid." She reached in her back pocket and took out her Bic lighter and gave it to Cindy. "Keep this in case we're gone a long time. If it gets dark, and cold, you can always build a fire."

"If Klandor has ordered elves to shoot on sight," Pan said, "then the road ahead will be equally dangerous. Perhaps I should go on alone."

"No," Adam said, coming to a fresh decision. "Sally and I will stay with you. You'll need our help with the wizard. Cindy will stay with Watch. Things will work out for the best. They always do."

Sally looked down at the wound in Watch's leg. "In all our adventures," she said anxiously, "this is the first time any of us has gotten seriously hurt. That worries me, it worries me a lot."

PAN FOUND THE CRYSTAL NECKLACE WITH-
out difficulty. As he had remembered, it was lying not
far from the road that led to his castle. Yet getting to
the necklace was hard and took more than two hours.
Because now they were afraid to walk openly on the
road. As a result they had to fight their way through
the trees, which took a lot of energy, even for Pan. By
the time Pan lifted the necklace out of the bushes, they
were all sweating and panting.

"It's not that impressive a piece," Sally said.

Pan brushed off the dirt. "Klandor had shined it up
that evening. I took a fancy to it."

"Let me see it," Adam said, stretching out his hand.

Pan gave it to him to hold. The gold chain was simple, thin links that could be found in any jeweler's shop. The crystals themselves were curious. There were three of them: two clear, like quartz crystals, and the other a deep blue, like a very large sapphire. What made them odd was that the clear ones were not set around the blue one. The blue stone was on the bottom, which threw off the color balance of the piece. Adam wondered if that was part of the reason it distorted one's mind. He was anxious to experiment with it and pulled the chain over his head, causing Sally to jump slightly.

"Are you sure you want to do that?" she asked. "Maybe the effect is permanent."

"Are you saying that my mind has been permanently distorted?" Pan asked, not pleased.

Sally spoke carefully. "I didn't know you before you used the crystal necklace," she said. "So I can't comment on that. But I do know that Adam has an extremely sensitive mind that is easily swayed. Why, the day he met Cindy Makey, he . . ."

"If we can't prove our theory," Adam interrupted, "then we may as well go home."

"But how are you going to tell if the necklace makes you see things opposite from the way you want them to be?" Sally asked. "When Pan used the necklace his emotions were involved. His very kingdom was at stake. You can't just pretend to get excited about wanting something to be a certain way. I doubt if it works that way."

Adam nodded. "I've been thinking about that. Yet there's something I want that I know I *really* want. I'm going to take a peek out on the road. And, Pan, don't tell me what I'm supposed to see. We'll just see if I see the opposite of what I really want and what is actually there. Do you understand?"

"No," Sally said. "Just hurry up and don't get shot."

Adam crept toward the open road. Searching up and down, he couldn't see any elves with bows and arrows. But his view was still shaded by the trees. He needed to get in the center of the road to have a good look around, to see what was up ahead. Taking a deep breath, he jumped out onto the wide path, the crystal necklace dangling around his neck.

Adam could not see Pan's castle.

There were just trees up ahead, endless trees.

But he did see a bunch of elves.

They leapt out of the woods, bows in hand.

Adam dashed back into the woods, back to his friends.

When he found them, he shook with fear.

"Did you see them?" he gasped. "They're coming."

"Who?" Sally asked.

"The elves. They're coming this way. We have to get out of here."

Pan peered through the trees. "I don't see anything."

Adam continued to tremble. "Are you sure?"

"I don't see anything either," Sally said, standing beside Pan.

Adam relaxed. "The elves weren't part of my test, but I was definitely right about this necklace. It makes you see the opposite of what you want to see."

"How can you be sure?" Sally asked.

"I'll answer that question in a second," Adam said. "But first, Pan, tell me how far we are from your castle right now?"

"Less than half a mile," Pan said.

"And when I stood in the middle of the road, should I have been able to see it?" Adam asked.

"Yes. It's a big castle. You should have seen it plainly."

Adam smiled. "But I didn't, and I really wanted to see it. I didn't have to fake that desire. We're all anxious to get there and confront Klandor and get Pan's kingdom back. But all I saw were trees as far as I looked. Also, I saw the elves with their bows and arrows, and you guys say the elves were not there."

"But maybe we were wrong," Sally said. "Maybe we just missed them."

"I don't think so," Adam said. "The crystal worked on either my mind or my eyes or both together to make me see something that wasn't there, and to take away something that was." He paused and looked up at Pan. "That night, at your party, you won many of the coin tosses. You just thought you lost every one because you were afraid to lose each time, and because you were wearing this necklace."

Pan's face darkened. "I thank you for your insight, Adam, and I admire your bravery to test that insight. I see now that what you say is true and I have to tell you that the truth has set my blood boiling. All this time I blamed myself for my foolishness. Now I see that even though I was foolish, I was cheated as well." His nostrils flared as he glanced in the direction of his castle. "I am going to race to my palace with this necklace and throw it in Klandor's face. I will demand that he return my kingdom immediately."

"No," Adam said quickly. "We must come with you. The wizard might trick you again."

Pan shook his head. "I cannot wait any longer now that I know the truth. My temper has been stirred, and it has been ages since that happened. Go back to Watch, to Cindy, and care for them. Return to your own world. I will take care of Klandor."

"Much as I would like to go home right now," Sally said, "I think Adam is right. You might need our help. You have to wait for us."

"You don't want to go out on the open road anyway," Adam said. "There might be elves there."

But Pan would not be talked into patience. He drew out his pipes and sucked in a deep breath. As he placed his lips to the pipes, earth-shaking notes pierced the woods. They went on for over a minute and both Adam and Sally had to cover their ears to keep from going deaf. But it was a song of some kind, primitive and haunting, and it stirred deep feelings inside each of them. When he was finished, Pan put aside the pipes and smiled proudly.

"Now all who hide in these woods will know that Pan has returned to reclaim his kingdom," he said. "No more will I crawl to my castle through the sheltering trees. I will go openly, and if you insist on accompanying me, then you must do the same. You must ride on my back."

Adam swallowed, stunned by the transformation in Pan. No longer was he the defeated creature hiding in the woods with his head bent low. Now he was like a fabled creature of old, filled with power and determination.

"Can you support both of us?" Adam asked.

In response Pan reached down and lifted them onto his back with one strong sweep of his arm. "I could carry you to the top of the highest peak," he said. "Now hold on tight. From here to the castle we fly with the wind. Nothing will stop us."

"Except for maybe a couple of arrows in the heart," Sally muttered as they leapt onto the road and thundered toward the castle, which stood less than a half mile in front of them. Sally added, "Now the wizard definitely knows we're coming."

9

WHEN PAN HAD OPERATED ON WATCH, HE had not only removed the arrow but covered the wound with a large green leaf coated with soothing herbs. Pan said the herbs would not only help with the pain, but would also keep infections from forming. The leaf was tied to Watch's leg with a strip torn from Cindy's shirt sleeve. Cindy had offered them her shirt while Pan was working on Watch. It disturbed her to look at it now, stained with her friend's blood. Watch noted her concern and patted her on the arm.

"Don't worry," he said, leaning back against a tree. "It's not as bad as it looks."

Cindy shook her head. "You're trying to act brave. I know it must hurt awful."

"It does hurt," Watch admitted. "But the herbs Pan put over the cut are working. They have made the torn flesh slightly numb."

"Pan must know a lot about plants," Cindy said.

"He's so ancient—he must know a lot about everything. I'm surprised he was so easily fooled by the wizard."

"I'm not surprised," she said. "Gambling brings out the worst in people. It makes them lose all sense. It's a twisted emotion—the desire to get something for nothing."

"I won't invite you to our next card game," Watch said.

Cindy smiled. "I didn't mean to sound so serious. Your card games are always fun." She paused. "But you know what always amazes me. You always win."

"That's because I cheat," he said. "The cards are marked. I marked them."

Cindy was astounded. "You're lying, you would never cheat anyone. I know you."

Watch explained. "I originally marked them because my eyes were so lousy that I couldn't even see what cards the rest of you discarded. In other words, I did it to make the game even. But since the witch improved my eyesight, I don't really need the marking to help my game. But I use them out of habit—so I never lose." He paused. "When we get back to Spooksville I promise I'll buy a fresh deck of cards."

Cindy laughed softly. "We don't play for money, so it's not really gambling." She stopped and looked around. "I wonder how the others are getting along."

"I bet they're at the castle already."

"Do you think they'll defeat the evil wizard?"

Watch shook his head. "Pan is not going to be able to storm into the castle and demand his kingdom back. The wizard will have guards, plenty of elementals that will have gone over to his side."

Cindy was worried. "Do you think they'll all be killed?"

"I think they need a good plan. I just hope Adam comes up with one before they come face to face with Klandor."

A small voice spoke nearby.

"Hello," it said.

Cindy leapt to her feet. "Who's there?"

"Who are you?" the voice asked softly.

Cindy and Watch looked all around. "Come out and show yourself," Cindy ordered.

"No," the voice said. "You have to tell me who you are first."

Cindy glanced anxiously at Watch, who simply shrugged. Cindy continued to scan the surrounding foliage, looking for a sign of their visitor.

"I'm Cindy," she said finally. "This is Watch. Who are you?"

"My name is Sarshi."

"Where are you?" Cindy asked. "Why can't we see you?"

"Because I don't want you to see me." Sarshi paused. "Are you human beings?"

"Yes," Cindy said. "What are you?"

"Don't you know?"

"No," Cindy said.

"Don't you want to guess?"

"Why should we guess?" Watch asked.

"Because if you guess right I might show myself to you."

"You're an elf," Cindy said.

"No."

"You're a leprechaun," Watch said.

"No. Guess again."

"You're a fairy," Cindy said.

Sarshi sounded disappointed. "How did you guess?"

"We were running out of names for elementals," Watch said. "Are you really a fairy?"

"Yes."

"Oh no," Cindy moaned. "I don't know if I can take another spell right now."

"I won't cast a spell on you," Sarshi said. "I don't want to hurt you."

"Why are you here?" Cindy asked.

"There is a rumor in the woods that Pan has returned. Another fairy told me that he has come with human kids. When I saw you I thought you might be with Pan."

"We were with him," Cindy explained. "But Watch was shot in the leg by an elf, and I stayed behind to guard him. Pan has gone along with our other friends."

"Be careful," Watch warned in a quiet voice. "This fairy might be on Klandor's side."

"I do not like Klandor," Sarshi replied. "I never do a thing he says. I am on Pan's side."

"But if you follow Pan," Cindy said, "how come you didn't follow him into our world? Why are you still here?"

Sarshi was a long time in answering. "Because these are my trees. This is my home. And I knew that one day Pan would return with an army and throw down Klandor."

Cindy had to smile. "He didn't bring much of an army I'm afraid. Our other friends are all he's got with him." She paused. "I do believe you are a nice fairy, and I hope you can tell we're nice humans. Would you please show yourself now?"

"OK. But you have to promise not to laugh at me."

"Why would we laugh?" Cindy asked.

"Because I am a kid fairy," Sarshi said, and with those words a tiny female figure appeared beside Cindy. She was at most half Cindy's height. Like the fairy they had met outside the dwarfs' cave, she wore a long dark coat and had bright green eyes. Only this fairy's hair was black, curly, and her tiny face was more cute than beautiful. On each of her ten fingers shone a glittering ring, each a different color and design. She stared up at Cindy with a smile so sweet it melted Cindy's heart. "Hello," Sarshi said.

Cindy offered her hand. "Pleased to meet you."

Sarshi stared at her hand. "What do you want me to do with your fingers?"

"In our culture," Cindy explained, "it is customary to shake hands when you meet someone new."

"You want to shake my hands?" Sarshi asked, puzzled.

"Just one hand would be enough," Watch said.

"Will you shake it hard?" Sarshi asked. "Will it hurt?"

Cindy dropped her hand. "We don't have to do it if you don't want to."

But Sarshi sounded disappointed. "Maybe we could

shake later." She glanced at Watch's injured leg and frowned. "The elves should not have shot at you, especially if you were with Pan. That was naughty of them."

"Are there elves still around here?" Cindy asked.

"No," Sarshi said with a twinkle in her eyes. "I led them away from here."

"How did you do that?" Watch asked.

Sarshi acted indignant. "I may be a small fairy but I am a powerful one." She spoke in an excited confidential tone. "I confused them with a magical spell. They thought they were chasing a bunch of dwarfs, when they were just chasing little old me."

"We're grateful you got them out of here," Cindy said.

Sarshi nodded to Watch's leg. "Does it hurt?"

"Only when I breathe," Watch said.

"Do you want me to heal you?" Sarshi asked.

"What do you mean?" Cindy asked.

Sarshi was confused. "You don't understand this simple question?"

"We're surprised at it," Cindy explained. "Can you really heal such a serious wound?"

Again Sarshi affected a proud air. "You think I'm just a kid."

"You said you were just a kid," Watch reminded her.

"Yes, that is true," Sarshi admitted. "But I am much

older than you two. I know from my mother that humans are not kids for long before they turn into something horrible she calls adults."

Cindy giggled. "They're not all horrible. How old are you? In human years?"

Sarshi cleared her throat. "I am one hundred and seventy-six of your years."

"No way," Watch said.

Sarshi looked suitably crushed. "Well, I am almost twenty of your years old."

"What does almost mean?" Cindy asked.

Sarshi lowered her head. "I'm ten years old."

"You're almost as old as us," Cindy said. "We can be friends. But as your friends, we don't want to take advantage of you. But if you can heal Watch's leg, we would appreciate it. You see we've been sitting in this forest for a long time now and we're getting hungry."

Sarshi brightened. "Why didn't you tell me? I know many food-making spells. What would you like to eat first?"

"*After* you fix my leg," Watch said, "I'd like a Spam sandwich with sprouts."

Sarshi frowned. "I don't know if I know a spell for Spam."

"A cheese sandwich would do just fine," Cindy said.

She added, "But if you can rustle up a chocolate cake for us, we would be eternally grateful."

"And a carton of milk," Watch added. "Can't eat cake without milk."

Sarshi nodded at Watch's wound. "Take off your bandage and let me see what those elves did to you. Pan may be a great king, and an OK doctor, but he is no fairy. I'll have you fixed up in a few minutes and then we can have a feast."

"Then can we go after our friends?" Cindy asked.

Sarshi was uncertain. "Klandor is a powerful wizard, stronger than any fairy. If he catches us, he will probably kill us." Then she added, "But I'll go with you to the castle. I'm tired of Klandor running things. I'll help in any way that I can."

10

PAN'S CASTLE WAS MAGNIFICENT. BUILT OF huge gray stones, it towered over them as they rode up on Pan's back, heading for the massive front entrance. There were guards, of course, grim dwarfs and humorless elves. They flanked the drawbridge that spanned the moat separating the castle from the rest of the countryside.

Each of these guards was armed. The dwarfs carried swords and hammers, the elves bows and arrows and knives. They stared tensely at Pan as he galloped up with Adam and Sally, but Pan's gaze was just as hard and fierce. Clearly he scared them—none of them thought to draw a weapon, but let Pan pass straight into the inner courtyard. Sally breathed a sigh of relief.

CHRISTOPHER PIKE

"I thought we were goners," she said.

"There's plenty of time for that," Adam said.

Sally nodded, knowing Pan wasn't even paying attention to them. He hadn't spoken to them once on the wild ride to the castle. He was so intent on having a showdown with the wizard that he wasn't thinking what he was going to do when it came. Adam said as much to Sally, who agreed.

"Klandor will just deny everything," she said.

"He will probably do worse than that," Adam said.

"Do you think we'll be killed?"

"I don't think he's going to roll out the red carpet." Adam paused. "I wish I could get Pan to slow down and consider what to do next."

"Talk to him."

"I tried."

"Talk to him again. It's our lives that are at stake."

Adam gently poked Pan in the back of his neck. "Pan," he said carefully. "Can we have a word with you?"

"Hmm," Pan muttered, distracted, as they strode through the courtyard. Along the high walls were more guards—dwarfs and elves—who had deserted Pan to follow the evil wizard. "What do you want?"

"It's about Klandor," Adam said. "He must know by now that you're on your way."

Pan was brisk. "I want him to know. Let the stinking wizard tremble on his staff."

"But what are you going to do about him?" Adam asked.

"What do you mean?" Pan asked impatiently.

"What he means is that Klandor is not going to welcome you with open arms," Sally explained. "Or us for that matter. We need a strategy."

Pan waved the crystal necklace "I have this as proof. He cheated me out of my own kingdom, plain and simple. He is to return it immediately or else."

"Or else what?" Adam asked hopefully.

Pan made a mean face. "Or else he will feel my wrath."

"That's what we wanted to talk to you about," Adam said. "This wrath of yours. It won't do you much good if you have nothing to back it up."

Pan snickered. "I can take Klandor any day, anytime."

"I'm sure you can," Sally said diplomatically. "And we wouldn't be worried if this was going to be a one-on-one contest. But if you haven't noticed, Pan, Klandor controls this castle. He has plenty of elves and dwarfs backing him up. I don't know if you can handle all of them at once."

Pan was not impressed. "They wouldn't dare hurt us."

"Actually," Adam said, "they've already shot one of

us. We mustn't underestimate them. You said it your-self, they have sworn allegiance to the wizard. If he tells them to grab us, they will."

Pan nodded grimly. They may have gotten to him a bit.

Yet he remained stubborn.

"I won't give him the chance," Pan swore.

They were inside the castle only two seconds when they were surrounded by a dozen dwarfs and elves. Each car-ried a long spear, which was pointed at Pan and his friends with significant effect. Pan couldn't just push them aside, and because he couldn't, his temper grew worse.

"You're my subjects!" he hollered. "I am your king! Get out of my way!"

They did clear a path of sorts for him. But they only gave Pan enough room to move forward; the spears didn't come down. If anything the tips were brought closer. A sharp point brushed Sally's ribs and she squealed.

"Ouch!" she said, and then she complained to Adam. "Why do we let ourselves get roped into these situa-tions? The next time a supernatural creature appears who needs help defeating the forces of darkness, we should just say, 'No, we're too busy. We have better things to do with our time.'"

Adam shook his head. "You know we can't turn down a friend in need."

"But Pan isn't a friend," she said in an anxious whisper. "We only just met him today. Maybe we can explain that to the wizard. Maybe we can tell him that Pan has, in reality, kidnapped us."

"You can't say that."

"Why not?"

"Because it's not true," Adam said.

"Who cares about the truth? We're talking about our lives here. If we have to lie to save ourselves, we should do it."

Adam was grim. "I doubt the wizard will believe any of our lies."

They were ushered into a vast room. The design was elaborate; there were many statues and exquisite paintings on the stone walls. Adam suspected it was here that Pan had his fateful celebration. At the end of the long room was a throne that had been Pan's, but now it belonged to the evil wizard, Klandor.

Even seated he was tall—as wizards usually were— and old and wrinkled. His skin was very pale and leathery; it looked as if he had never seen the sun, and that if he laughed, even once, his expression would crack into something more awful than it already was. He wore a ragged purple robe; it looked as if the blood of many past enemies had been spilled on it. But it was his eyes that were the real horror—tiny and black, beads spun at night by spiders who ate their victims alive.

These eyes followed them as they were carefully escorted to the throne. On top of Klandor's old head was a pointed red and black cap. The colors on it moved as Adam stared at it, flowing currents of danger. The cap was a storage container of energy to fuel the wizard's evil magic.

Pan was brought within thirty feet of the throne before Klandor raised his hand. The spears converged to stop Pan. Adam noticed then how long the wizard's nails were, how sharp and darkly stained, as if they had been dipped in blood. Klandor leaned forward in his seat and held up a bony finger.

"You were banished from my kingdom," he said in a scratchy voice that carried disturbing authority. It sent a chill deep into Adam's bones. "Why have you returned?"

Pan held up the crystal necklace. "You know why I have returned! You lied to me the night I won this necklace. You said it was merely decoration, something that complemented my horns. What you did not say was that it was a magical device designed to twist the vision of the one who wears it. I did not lose all those many times to you. I won often, and sitting across from me, you knew that I won. But you cheated me and forced me to risk everything to steal my kingdom, a kingdom that still belongs to me!"

Klandor smiled, his lips a thin, straight line, and the many wrinkles on his face crowded so tightly together that it was as if his skin were covered with spiders' webs. He looked more than old then, more like something that had been dead for weeks and only brought back to life with the power of forbidden spells and unthinkable sacrifices. His black eyes shone with a cold light as his hideous smile widened. Adam had the feeling that he was not impressed by the fact that Pan had just called him a liar and a thief.

"I forced you to do nothing," Klandor said. "You were mad that night, so puffed up with your pride and position that you didn't know when to stop. In front of a hundred witnesses you gambled away your kingdom. Everyone saw, everyone knows the truth. Now you enter my home and insult me with your lies. You try to rewrite what was. How should I reward such behavior, Pan? Perhaps I was too kind to allow you and your miserable followers to leave this land in peace. For it does not seem that you have returned in peace. Yes, I know about the four human warriors you have brought with you to assassinate me. I see you have two of them on your back. Wretched creatures they look to me, and unworthy of being even in your questionable company. Have they anything to say for themselves?"

"Yeah," Sally spoke up. "First of all, I resent being referred to as a wretched creature. Now, it is true that from time to time I suffer from bad moods, and on such occasions it could be said that I am wretched. But that is a momentary state of mind and doesn't constitute my true nature. In other words, it's not fair to label me wretched. Especially when the label is being applied by the likes of you, since you are obviously a down-on-his-luck magician who couldn't get a decent gig at a Chamber of Commerce breakfast." Sally paused and then suddenly jerked to the side. "Ouch! Adam? Why did you poke me in the side?"

"Because I think I should talk to him instead of you," he whispered.

"What am I doing wrong?" she asked.

"I thought you were going to try to reason with him?"

"But you told me not to lie!"

"Not all reason is a lie," Adam reminded her.

"You can't reason with an evil wizard," Sally whispered back.

"I can try." Adam cleared his throat and spoke to

Klandor. "As you can see, Mr. Klandor, we're friends of Pan. We don't deny that, although we just met him this afternoon while we were trying to find our bikes in the forest. But we're not assassins. We didn't come here to kill you. We don't believe in killing, especially if it could get us killed. But we do believe Pan has a point when he says he was conned out of his kingdom. Now, I tested this necklace and I discovered that it definitely alters how one sees the world. And I know if Pan was wearing it when he gambled his kingdom away, then he was playing with an unfair disadvantage. Now, what I think you two should do is retire to a nice quiet place and talk about how—"

"Silence!" Klandor shouted, raising his bony hand again. "You have the nerve to accuse me of being a cheat in front of all my loyal subjects?"

"Well," Adam said carefully, "I didn't use the word *cheat.*"

"But he did imply it," Sally added. "Because you did cheat Pan. You cheated him because you're a natural born loser. Just look at the company you keep—all these half-baked dwarfs and elves. Why, I've seen leprechauns with chocolate cakes for treasure that could take this lousy company."

"Sally," Adam said.

"What?"

"Please do not speak again until we are back in Spooksville and there are no sharp spears pointed at us."

"Like you had a lot of success calling him a cheat," Sally snapped.

"You are going to get us killed."

"Then at least I'll die with my tongue working, which is all that matters."

Adam sighed. "Oh brother."

Pan spoke up, and his temper was no less for having listened to the ramblings of the rest of them. "Klandor!" he shouted, waving the necklace again. "You were always good with words, but let's see how good you are with a sword. Right now, in front of all these traitors you call loyal subjects, I challenge you to one-on-one combat. If truth is on your side, you will surely defeat me. But if you refuse to fight, then all will know the reason why. Because you are not only a cheat and a liar, but a coward as well!"

Sally looked at Adam. "He's worse than both of us."

"Shh," Adam cautioned.

Klandor chuckled long and wickedly. "You come here swearing challenges of honor and bravery. You, who have not even a place to hang your horns. You're not a king anymore, Pan. You have no right to challenge a true king, like myself. But because I am a king I know the meaning of mercy. My loyal servants are going to once again escort you from my land. Should you try to return, though, should we see your face ever again, you will be slaughtered and eaten by those who strike you down. Goat meat is a delicacy in these parts. As to your insolent human friends, they are to remain here with me, where I will do with them what I wish. And as to the crystal necklace you won from me, I will let you keep it. Let it be a reminder to you of how far you have fallen."

Sally looked at Adam again. "I told you how evil he was."

Adam sighed. "I'm afraid you were right."

11

CINDY, WATCH, AND SARSHI RAN INTO PAN about midway between the castle and the interdimensional portal. Cindy and Watch were concerned that Adam and Sally weren't with Pan. But when they questioned Pan about their friends' whereabouts, Pan merely hung his head low and acted depressed. It was then they noticed that he wore a crystal necklace. Both Cindy and Watch wondered if it was the one that was responsible for all the trouble. But it was difficult to get any information out of Pan.

"At least tell us if they're still alive," Cindy said, exasperated.

Pan finally looked up at that. "I'm sorry, Cindy. The

last time I saw them they were alive, but I don't know what Klandor has done to them by now. The wizard has absolutely no honor. In front of everyone I explained exactly how he had cheated me, and he had the nerve to deny it. Then, when I challenged him to combat, he refused to cross swords with me. He is not only evil, he is unethical."

"Like all this is a big surprise to us," Watch said.

Cindy was anxious. "We have to get back to the castle. We have to rescue Adam and Sally before he does something horrible to them."

Pan shook his head. "It is impossible. If I go back there, I will be killed and eaten. And you'll never get into the castle without me to lead you."

"Excuse me," Cindy said angrily, "Adam and Sally risked their lives to help you. Now you had better risk your life to save them. We are going back to the castle and you are going with us. That is a fact you'd better accept right now."

Pan appeared crushed. "Fine. But we will be walking to our deaths." He sighed and gazed up at the sky. "Not that I would mind leaving this world right now."

Watch nodded to the crystal necklace. "Is that the piece that we've heard so much about?"

Pan glanced down. "Yes. I was just about to throw it away again."

Watch held out his hand. "May I see it?"

Pan gave it to him. "You may keep it. I would rather not have to see it again in this life."

"Hello, Pan," Sarshi said.

Pan frowned in her direction. "Who are you?"

"A fairy. A loyal subject. I am here to help save your kingdom."

"How old are you?" Pan asked.

Sarshi fidgeted. "Almost ten. But I'm very powerful. Just ask Watch. I healed his leg."

"She fixed it up better than you had," Watch admitted as he studied the crystal necklace. "I don't even have a limp. She also fed us." Watch pointed out the order of the stones to Cindy. "See how the blue one is set at the bottom."

"So what?" Cindy said. "What does it mean?"

Watch shrugged. "I don't know. But it would look prettier if the clear stones were set on either side of the blue one."

"But who cares whether it's pretty or not?" Cindy asked. "All that matters is whether we can use it as a weapon to get back at Klandor and free Adam and Sally."

Watch spoke to Pan. "Did Adam certify that this thing makes you see the opposite of what you desire?"

"I think so," Pan mumbled.

"Yes or no?" Cindy demanded.

"Yes," Pan replied. "It turns the whole brain upside down."

Watch considered. "What if we could convince Klandor to gamble with us? What if when we do so, we have Sarshi secretly slip this necklace around the wizard's neck? We might be able to trick him with his own tool."

"What do we have to offer him that he will want to gamble with us?" Cindy asked.

Watch touched his pants pocket. "I have a thing or two with me that he might desire."

"But I told you," Sarshi said, "Klandor is more powerful than any fairy. I can weave an invisible net around myself, but his keen eyes will pierce it. He will see me if I try to slip the necklace around his neck, and he will know what we're up to."

"I've thought about that." Watch fiddled with the bottom blue stone. "Still, it may be possible to distract him somehow so that you can do what you need to do. To make him believe he knows what we're up to and have him be completely wrong."

"What are you talking about?" Cindy asked.

Watch pulled the blue stone free. "I think the order of these crystals is important." He held the stone up to the light. "In fact, I think the order makes the whole thing work."

12

AFTER PAN LEFT, KLANDOR TURNED ADAM and Sally into chickens. Adam became a rooster and Sally a hen. Klandor simply waved his bony arms and chanted a few nasty words and the transformation occurred, right in front of all the elves and dwarfs, who cheered the spectacle. Then the wizard ordered that the two be taken outside and put in the wire cage with the other poultry. It seemed Klandor planned on having chicken for dinner that night.

Adam and Sally huddled in a corner of the cage and tried to look inconspicuous. The other chickens walked around and pecked at the seed spread on the ground. So far Adam and Sally had not invited much attention. Normally Adam wouldn't have looked twice at the seed, but now it did seem kind of appealing. He hadn't had lunch. He told Sally as much.

"How can you think of eating at a time like this?" she snapped at him. "We have to get out of here and get back to the others."

"If we do get back to the others," Adam said, "they might eat us."

Sally was worried. Adam had never seen a worried chicken before, and the sight would have been comical if the situation had been less dire.

"But we can still speak," Sally said. "We can talk to them. They'll recognize us that way."

"We seem to be speaking to each other," Adam said, "but we don't have human vocal cords. I doubt a person would understand us. In fact, I suspect we sound no different from all the other chickens gathered here."

"That's depressing," Sally said.

"It's reality."

Sally was annoyed. "How can you say being turned into chickens is reality? Nothing in this dimension makes any sense. We have to figure out a way out of here, I tell you, and soon."

"You're not listening to me. Getting out of here is only half our problem. We still have to get Klandor to change us back into human beings. And I don't know how we can do that. The guy is completely unreasonable."

"Like calling him a cheat was reasoning with him."

"I didn't say that," Adam said. "You said that. And probably if you had kept your mouth shut, we would be with Pan right now, walking back toward the portal."

"Pan's a loser," Sally grumbled. "Klandor says he can go, so he just leaves. He hardly says goodbye to us. I swear, the wizard should have changed him into something."

"He does have half a goat's body already," Adam remarked.

"So put a penguin head on him. What I mean is, it was his kingdom that we were trying to win back and he's the one who gets set free. It's not fair."

"When has Spooksville ever been fair?" Adam asked.

Sally fumed, which made her feathers stand up straighter. "We're a long way from Spooksville right now."

That point was driven home a moment later when a fat white hen came up to Adam and started nudging his side. Adam tried to push the hen away, but the creature kept pressing against him, much to his annoyance.

"I think she likes you," Sally observed.

"Don't be ridiculous," Adam said.

"Why are you embarrassed?" Sally asked. "You have nice red feathers, cool skinny legs. I find you kind of cute myself."

"I am not a rooster," Adam replied. "Don't treat me like one."

"You're the one who just said we have to face reality," Sally said. "Right now, you look like a rooster." She added, "Do you think I'm a good-looking hen?"

"I wouldn't know a good-looking hen if one was staring me in the face," Adam said. The fat white chicken finally got on his nerves. Using all his strength, he pushed it away. But the creature just jumped back to his side. "What's your problem?" Adam asked.

The hen replied. "I love you."

Adam blinked. "What?"

Sally burst out laughing. "Oh my! Adam has a girlfriend!"

Adam yelled at her. "Shut up! Don't let the other chickens hear that. This one is bad enough. Anyway, this hen doesn't love me. It's just a chicken. It's not even supposed to be able to talk."

The fat hen brushed up against Adam again.

"You are such a strong rooster," she said.

Sally was dying with laughter. She appeared to be on the verge of shedding all her feathers simultaneously.

"She'll want to have your eggs next, Adam!" she howled. "You better tell her that you only work for the Easter Bunny!"

Adam fumed. "This is not funny!"

"This is outrageous!" Sally told him.

The fat hen continued to pester him.

"How come I haven't seen you around before?" she asked.

"I'm—I'm not from these parts," Adam mumbled.

The fat hen leaned close. "Are you happy here?"

Adam averted his head. "No. I am not happy."

"Why not?" the hen asked, standing so close to Adam that he could feel her chicken breath on his feathers. But then Adam got an idea.

"I'm not happy because I'm sick," he said. "I have a fatal illness."

The fat hen drew back a step. "What's wrong with you?"

Sally had yet to stop laughing.

"I have an allergy," Adam said.

"But allergies are not fatal," the hen said.

"This one is," Adam said. "I'm allergic to feathers. Especially white ones. Just being around you is killing me."

The fat hen looked sad. "Do you want me to go away?"

"Yes, please," Adam said. "Go as far away as possible."

"But will we meet again?"

"Only time will tell," Adam said.

Dejected, the fat hen wandered off. Sally poked Adam in the ribs, or rather, in the white meat part of the breast. She had finally begun to calm down.

"Why didn't you just tell her you were with me?" she asked.

"I don't think chickens respect committed relationships."

Sally was impressed. "Is that what we have? Now that Cindy will no longer be interested in you?"

Adam brushed her off. An elf was walking toward the metal cage, and he had a couple of bags in his hand. Adam pointed him out.

"This is our chance to escape," he said.

Sally shook with fear. "Don't be ridiculous. That elf is coming for dinner."

"Can we stay here forever?" Adam asked. "We have to get out of this cage. Once back in the castle we might have room to maneuver."

"Once we're in the castle they'll eat us," Sally cried. "Please, Adam, we can't let him catch us. I'm claustrophobic. I can't be stuffed in a bag. I'm attached to my head. I can't stand the thought of having it separated from my shoulders."

But Adam had made up his mind. "I would rather die

than be hit on by fat chickens for the rest of my life." He took a step toward the elf as the servant of the wizard began to open the cage. "Come with me, Sally. It will be all right."

"I hope they don't fry me." Sally moaned. "I can't stand fried chicken."

13

PAN HAD SOMEHOW BLUFFED HIS WAY BACK into the castle. But this time when he was brought before Klandor in the huge hall—with Watch and Cindy beside him—the wizard appeared more frightening than before. The mood inside the castle was grim. Once upon a time these dwarf and elf guards had served Pan. Few of them disliked Pan. They had gone over to Klandor's side for business reasons. It was nothing personal. The wizard had the power now, that was all that mattered.

No doubt that was the reason Klandor had allowed Pan to go free. The wizard hadn't wanted to push Pan's once-loyal subjects too far, and possibly set off an uprising.

In fact, the elves and dwarfs that had been sent to escort Pan to the interdimensional portal had let him go free a mile from the castle. They hadn't wanted to rub salt in their ex-master's obvious wounds. But Klandor had laid down the law with Pan only a few hours before, in front of everyone, and now Pan had chosen to violate it. Klandor could not let him go again without losing face. For that reason the first words out of the wizard's mouth were scary indeed.

"Do you have any last words, Pan?" he asked.

Pan had regained a measure of strength. "Yes. My friends want to play a game with you."

The reply momentarily stunned Klandor, but he recovered quickly. "What kind of game?" he asked.

"They want to gamble with you," Pan explained. "Toss the coin, as we tossed the coin."

Klandor laughed softly, deadly. "What do they have to wager that I could possibly want?"

"These," Watch said, pulling his pocket calculator and Sally's Bic lighter from his pocket. "This calculator is actually a miniature computer. It can perform every type of mathematical calculation imaginable. It can also store data related to one's personal calendar. You can write yourself reminder notes. Although the keyboard is tiny, you can even write a love letter or a whole term paper using this instrument."

Klandor tried to act disinterested, although it was obvious he was intrigued. "What's the warranty on it?"

"Two years, parts and labor," Watch said.

"What's its power source?" Klandor asked.

"Two triple-A batteries."

The wizard snorted. "Where am I going to get batteries in this dimension? The calculator will just run down and then be useless to me."

"That's true," Watch admitted. "But it has fresh lithium batteries in it right now. If you use the calculator carefully, it will take ages before the batteries go dead."

Klandor considered. "What else have you brought?"

Watch held aloft the lighter, flicked it a couple of times so the flame appeared and disappeared. "This lighter is brand-new," he said. "Its fuel reserve is at maximum. But even when it does run out, even in this dimension, you should be able to replenish it with another source of fuel."

Klandor acted unimpressed. "I'm a powerful wizard. I can start a fire by snapping my fingers. What do I need a lighter for?"

"Excuse me for putting it this way," Watch said. "But you're an old powerful wizard, and you ain't getting younger. I bet starting a fire isn't as easy as it used to be. But with this lighter in your pocket, you won't even have to remember the spell for fire."

"Are you questioning my memory, young human?" Klandor snapped.

"Not at all," Watch said. "But as the years roll by, all of us have a little more trouble remembering the most obvious facts. All I'm saying is that the lighter and the calculator make living life that much easier and pleasanter." He paused. "These are the two items we have brought to wager. Two items, I believe, that are difficult, if not impossible, to obtain in this dimension."

Klandor considered. "What do you want me to wager in return?"

Watch didn't hesitate. "Your wizard's hat for the lighter."

"Is that all?" Klandor asked.

Watch shrugged. "It's a nice hat. I want it."

"You want it because it's a magical hat," Klandor said sternly. "It is worth far more than your silly lighter."

"That's my offer. Take it or leave it."

"I'll make you a counteroffer," the wizard said. "Both the lighter and the calculator for my hat."

Watch shook his head. "No dice."

Klandor smiled thinly. "We won't use dice. We toss a coin. Heads or tails. It is very simple. You either win or you lose." He paused. "You must wager both."

"No," Watch said.

"What are you saving the calculator for?"

"A second wager."

"What do you want for it?" Klandor asked.

"That is none of your business. Not unless you win both items from me."

The wizard scowled. "You are a stubborn human."

"We are a stubborn race," Cindy chipped in.

Klandor waved his hand. "All right, I will put up my hat for the lighter. I will even let you toss the coin and let you call it while it is still in the air. Does that sound fair?"

"Yes," Watch replied, bringing out the crystal necklace. "The only condition I have is that you wear this necklace while we play."

Every dwarf and elf in the room leaned in closer.

Pan smiled slightly although he remained silent.

Klandor was suspicious. "Why should I wear it?"

"Why not?" Cindy asked. "You say it has no effect on the wearer."

"I must insist that you wear it if you want to win this fine lighter and this superb calculator," Watch said. "Our good friend Pan had to wear it before, and now it's your turn."

"I did not force Pan to wear the necklace," Klandor said. "He chose to wear it."

"Is there some reason you are afraid to wear it?" Cindy taunted gently.

The wizard snorted. "I am afraid of nothing." He stood up from his throne. "Give me the necklace. Loyal slaves, get my pillow and gold coin." He rubbed his hands together as if he were eager for the contest to begin. "Step forward and lay out your goods, Watch. This will be the last time you see them."

A few minutes later Watch was sitting opposite Klandor, with the whole assembly looking on. Many held their breath—the tension was that great. Yet Watch seemed unconcerned as he sat across from the evil wizard. Watch rubbed the gold coin between his fingers.

"Are you sure you don't want to toss it?" Watch asked. "I don't mind. That way there can be no possibility of my cheating you." He paused. "Does that sound fair?"

Klandor grabbed the gold coin from him. "You think to play with me, young human, but I warn you. I have played against much greater beings than you and I have beaten them every time."

"Then play. Toss the coin. Call it anyway you want."

Klandor glanced at the coin, at the crystal necklace around his neck, at the crowd. Once more a faint smile touched his lips. He gestured to a nearby dwarf to come closer.

"What is your name?" he asked the dwarf.

"Bartmeal," the dwarf said. Apparently the dwarf *could* speak, at least in the elemental kingdom.

"Bartmeal," Klandor said. "Once the coin lands, I want you to read out what it is to the audience. Heads or tails. You understand?"

The dwarf was uneasy. Obviously he worried that if he had to read out that it was tails, when his master had called for heads, he would be placed in a precarious position. The reverse could be equally compromising. Bartmeal was probably wondering if he would have a head on his shoulders when the day finally ended. Yet he was caught in a jam, and there was nothing he could do about it. He seemed to recognize that fact. He nodded his large head.

"I understand," Bartmeal said.

"I want you to tell the truth," Klandor emphasized.

Bartmeal nodded. "I will tell the truth, Master."

Watch yawned. "Can we get on with this, please?"

Klandor tossed the coin in the air.

"Tails," he called out.

It was heads. Bartmeal called out the word.

The assembly buzzed with noise.

Klandor sat astounded. Then he shouted at the group. "Be quiet!"

The gathering quieted down. Fast.

Klandor reached for his hat and handed it to Watch.

"You have won your prize," he said in a scratchy voice.

Watch smiled. "Would you like to win it back? The hat and the lighter? Double or nothing?"

Klandor was interested. His dark eyes flashed with a cold light.

"What do I have to wager?" he asked.

"The freedom of our two friends that you took hostage," Watch said. "I assume they are still alive?"

Klandor hesitated. "Yes, they are alive." He clapped his hands together. "Fine, it is a wager. Your friends for my hat and the lighter. But I toss the coin this time as well, and Bartmeal reads out what it is."

"I would have it no other way," Watch said.

Klandor tossed the coin in the air.

"Heads!" he called out.

It landed tails. Bartmeal whispered the word to the assembly.

"Louder please," Cindy called.

"It was tails," Bartmeal said, throwing his master an anxious look. Klandor fumed.

"You cheat me," he accused Watch.

Watch was the picture of innocence. "How do I cheat you? You control everything."

Klandor complained. "I don't know how you are doing it!"

"Is it the necklace?" Watch asked sympathetically. "Is it disturbing you in some way? I know you made it, but perhaps it is not as safe to wear as you thought. You can take it off now, if you like. I'm sure all those watching wouldn't mind."

Of course, Klandor could not remove the necklace. That would be the same as admitting it was rigged and admitting that Pan had indeed been cheated out of his kingdom. Klandor continued to fret.

"You have to give me a chance to win back what I have lost," he told Watch.

"Fine. We can go double or nothing again."

Klandor was wary. "What do I have to wager?"

"Just your castle."

"My castle! That's ridiculous. What makes you think I would wager all this just to win a few trinkets and the lives of your friends?"

Watch spoke smoothly, loud enough for all to hear. "Because you are a gambling wizard. Because you have never lost before. Because you are sure, this time, you can beat me." Watch paused. "Or have I really beaten you at your own game?"

The wizard's face flushed with blood. "I toss the coin again."

Watch shrugged. "As you wish."

Klandor tossed the coin in the air.

"Tails," he called.

It was heads. Bartmeal didn't look so good.

Nor did Klandor. "I can't give up my castle," he moaned.

Watch leaned forward. "I'll give you a chance to win it back. Double or nothing."

Klandor sat back. "What do I have to wager?"

"Everything."

"What do you mean?"

"Everything you took from Pan: his title, his castle, his kingdom. If you lose you must give it all back."

Klandor was insulted. "That's absurd. I would never wager that much."

"It's your choice," Watch said.

Klandor burned with indecision. Then he nodded his head vigorously.

"I have to win at least once," he said.

The wizard tossed the coin in the air.

"Tails!" Klandor screamed.

It was heads. Bartmeal fainted.

Klandor threw a fit. "I'm not giving up my kingdom! I'm not going back to being ignored by everyone!"

Pan stepped forward then and grabbed the wizard by the neck.

"You have no choice, Klandor," he said in a clear and strong voice. "Just as I had no choice."

Glancing around the room at the enthusiastic nods of the assembled dwarfs and elves, Watch and Cindy could see that everyone else agreed with Pan

Klandor was history.

But they still needed the wizard for one last thing.

Pan was naturally overjoyed to have his kingdom back and wanted to throw a huge feast to celebrate. But while they were waiting for the food to be prepared, a rooster and a hen suddenly flew through the hall. Apparently they had just escaped from the kitchen. Both birds were making an awful noise. Pan nodded to one of the armed elves.

"Shoot those birds down," he said. "We can have them for our meal."

The archer raised his bow and arrow.

"Wait!" Cindy screamed. "Don't shoot!"

The elf hesitated. Pan looked at Cindy.

"What's the matter?" he asked.

"That's Sally," she gasped. "The hen is Sally."

"But it's just a chicken," Watch said.

Cindy shook her head. "No, it's Sally, I'm positive. The rooster must be Adam. Klandor must have changed them into birds. Pan, we have to get the wizard out of your dungeon. He has to change them back."

"But how can you be so sure?" Pan asked.

Cindy smiled. "I would recognize Sally's squawk anywhere."

Epilogue

PAN WAS UNABLE TO ESCORT THEM BACK TO the interdimensional portal. He said he had too much work to do to get his kingdom in order so that he could invite the elementals to come home. Pan wished them his best as they said goodbye, however, and promised that their bikes and other stuff would be returned to them soon.

But cute little fairy Sarshi came along to keep them company. She walked between them as Watch explained his plan to Adam and Sally, who were still scratching at feathers that were no longer there.

"First I reversed the order of the stones in the crystal necklace," Watch said. "I discovered that when I did that, it didn't work at all."

"Then why did you insist Klandor wear it?" Adam asked.

"To confuse him. He expected to see everything the reverse of what he wanted. When that didn't happen during the coin tosses, he lost all his sense of balance."

"But why was that important?" Sally asked.

Watch explained. "To keep him distracted so that he wouldn't notice Sarshi hanging invisible in the air between us, tipping the coin at the last second so that it would always land the opposite of what he called out. I had him throw the coin for that same reason. The more he had to do, the less likely he was to notice what Sarshi was doing."

Sally patted Watch on the back. "You're a genius."

Watch was gracious. "Cindy contributed at least half the plan."

"No," Cindy said. "Ten percent, at most."

Adam patted Cindy on the back. "You're still a genius."

Cindy blushed. "Sarshi deserves most of the credit. After all, she was the one who had to stay invisible right in the face of a powerful wizard, and keep altering the coin as it fell on the pillow. I'm sure that was no easy trick. Isn't that right, Sarshi?"

The little fairy was embarrassed. "I have a confession to make."

"What?" Watch asked.

She hesitated. "I wasn't there."

Watch chuckled. "You're kidding."

"No," Sarshi said in a tiny voice. "I couldn't get my invisible web to work. I tried again and again but the spell kept failing." She added, "When you were gambling with the wizard, I was sitting in the back with the dwarfs, watching."

They were all shocked.

"But how could you have failed me?" Watch asked.

"Maybe I was too nervous." She added quietly, "To tell you the truth, I'm only nine years old."

Cindy burst out laughing. But Watch was still confused.

"But how did I win on every toss of the coin?" he asked.

"I don't know." Sarshi smiled sweetly. "Sometimes you just get lucky."

TURN THE PAGE FOR A SNEAK PEEK AT
SPOOKSVILLE #9: THE WISHING STONE

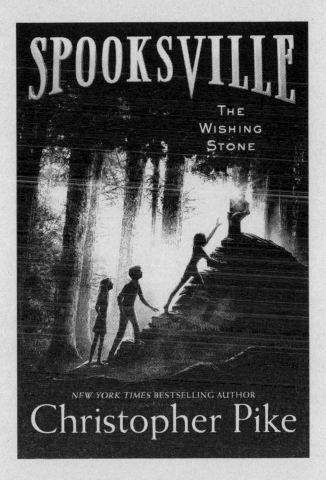

SALLY WILCOX SAW THE WISHING STONE first. For that reason she felt it belonged mainly to her. That was probably the same reason she suffered more than the others from the stone. The more that was asked of it, the more it demanded in return. Of course no one knew that at first. But even if Sally had known, she probably would have made the same wishes anyway. She was a strong-willed girl, and rather impulsive.

She and her three friends—Cindy Makey, Adam Freeman, and Watch—were not far outside of Spooksville, their hometown, when they first spotted the stone. Since dealing with Pan's leprechauns and fairies in the thick forest high in the hills overlooking the town, they had been staying closer to Spooksville, not wandering too deep into dangerous places that were hard to leave. However, no place in or around Spooksville was really safe. The gang was only hiking in the foothills when Sally stopped and pointed toward a sparkle in the trees, maybe a quarter of a mile off the path they were taking through a gully.

"What's that?" she asked, brushing aside her dark bangs.

"I don't see anything," Adam, who was shorter than the others, said.

"Neither do I," Watch said, removing his thick glasses and cleaning them on his shirtsleeve. "Did you see an animal?"

"No," Sally said, thoughtful. "It was a flash of light."

"It could have just been a reflection," Cindy said, standing behind them.

"Obviously," Sally said, leading the group. "But a reflection of what?" She paused. "I think we should look."

"I don't know," Cindy said, fingering her long blond hair. "If we go off the path, we'll get all dirty."

"And we might run into a strange animal and have our internal organs ripped from our bodies," Watch added.

Sally frowned at Watch. "And you used to be so adventurous," she said.

"I was younger then," Watch said.

"You're only twelve now," Adam observed. He nodded to Sally. "I'll go with you to check it out. It shouldn't take long to hike over there." Sally had pointed to the far side of the gully they were presently hiking through.

"We should probably all go together," Cindy said. "It's not safe to separate out here."

"It's not safe to be alive out here," Sally said.

"But it's better than being dead," Watch said.

They hiked in the direction of the supposed flash Sally had seen. When they reached the spot, they searched the area without seeing anything unusual.

"It was probably just a trick of light," Adam said.

"Perhaps some debris from a crashed flying saucer," Watch added.

But Sally was unconvinced. "It was a bright flash. There must be something strange out here."

"But strange is not necessarily good," Cindy said.

Sally looked at her. "Are you getting scared again?"

"Yes," Cindy said, and added sarcastically, "just being out in the wilderness with you makes me tremble in my shoes."

"Let's continue our hike," said Adam. "Then we can go and get some ice cream."

But Sally was unconvinced. "I want to search the

area one more time. I can do it myself. You guys rest here if you're tired."

In fact, they were all tired. The summer was almost over but obviously the sun didn't know. It was another hot, cloudless day. Adam, Cindy, and Watch plopped down on some boulders in the shade while Sally went off on her own. Cindy had brought a bottle of apple raspberry juice and passed it around.

"Another ten days and school starts," Watch said, taking a deep gulp of the juice and letting out a satisfied sigh. "We won't have many more days like this."

"We'll have the weekends free," Adam, who was new in town, said. "We'll have plenty of time to hang out and have fun."

Watch shook his head as he passed the juice to Adam. "You don't know the teachers in this town. They give you so much homework, you have to work all weekend."

"Why do they do that?" Cindy, who was also new, asked. "We don't all want to grow up to be rocket scientists."

"They just want to give us a chance to complete our studies," Watch said.

"But what's the hurry?" Adam asked.

Watch shrugged. "You've been here long enough to know the answer to that. Not that many kids live long enough to graduate. Last year only about a dozen people graduated from junior high, and half of them were missing body parts."

"What about the other half?" Adam asked reluctantly.

"Most of them were insane," Watch said.

Cindy grimaced. "That's horrible!"

"I don't know," Watch said. "They had a great all-night graduation party."

"I hope we get to be in a lot of classes together," Adam said.

Watch shook his head. "It might be better to separate. Then, if there is an explosion or something, at least one of us will survive."

"You have explosions at school?" Cindy asked. "I don't believe it."

"We had a half-dozen explosions last year. Most of them were in chemistry class. The teacher used to work for the CIA." Watch added, "But I think they got rid of him."

Suddenly they heard Sally shouting.

"I've found something! I've found something!"

About the Author

CHRISTOPHER PIKE is the author of more than forty teen thrillers, including the Thirst, Remember Me, and Chain Letter series. Pike currently lives in Santa Barbara, where it is rumored he never leaves his house. But he can be found online at ChristopherPikeBooks.com.